THE ROMAN MYSTERY SCROLLS

the
Thunder
Omen

Also by Caroline Lawrence

THE ROMAN MYSTERY SCROLLS

the Thunder Omen

CAROLINE LAWRENCE

Orion
Children's Books

First published in Great Britain in 2013
by Orion Children's Books
a division of the Orion Publishing Group Ltd
Orion House
5 Upper St Martin's Lane
London WC2H 9EA
An Hachette UK company

1 3 5 7 9 10 8 6 4 2

A catalogue record for this book is available from the British Library.

ISBN 978 1 4440 0457 1

Printed in Great Britain by Clays Ltd, St Ives plc

To Dr Helen Forte,
for her wonderful illustrations

SCROLL I

IT WAS EARLY MORNING ON THE FIRST day of the Saturnalia, the Roman mid-winter festival of gift-giving, feasting and dancing.

It was a topsy-turvy holiday when anything could happen.

In the port of Ostia, in a one-room shack behind a temple, eight sacred chickens were dancing on a table. Wearing tiny conical caps of different colours, they clucked happily and strutted in circles.

Threptus the soothsayer's apprentice stood beside the table. He was playing panpipes made from Tiber reeds and stamping his right foot to make a belled ankle-bangle jangle.

Threptus loved the Saturnalia.

Everyone wore colourful clothes and the cone-shaped caps that slaves put on when they were set free. Patrons did not receive clients, but sent them gifts instead. Boys did not have to go to school. Girls did not have to weave at the loom. Slaves did not have to work, and some even traded places with their masters.

Threptus was not a slave, and he liked being a soothsayer's apprentice, but he was looking forward to a week of fun, feasting and gifts.

On this special day, he wanted to wake his master in a special way: with the dance of the sacred chickens.

Still playing the panpipes and jangling his ankle-bangle, he dipped his free hand into an open sack on a low shelf and tossed a few grains of barley onto the table. The chickens eagerly gobbled up the treat and danced even harder.

'Bweerp, bweerp, bweerp!' they sang.

Fast asleep on a narrow bed against the raw plank wall, Floridius the Soothsayer snored contentedly.

From outside the one-roomed shack came a distant growl of thunder.

Threptus glanced nervously at a rectangular hole in the roof. This compluvium made the house delightfully cool in the summer, but in winter it let in the rain. On the table, the sacred chickens kept dancing, but their song of contentment was turning to clucks of alarm as the first drops of rain began to fall.

'Bk-bk-bk-bk-bk!'

Threptus wanted his master to see the hens before Jupiter drenched their spirits, so he took the panpipes from his mouth.

'Yo, Saturnalia!' he shouted, then quickly resumed playing and stamping his jangly ankle-bangle.

Floridius rolled over to face Threptus. Was he awake? No. His eyes were still closed and his lips flapped as he breathed out.

Once again, Threptus stopped playing just long enough to shout, 'Yo, Saturnalia!'

The rain was getting heavier. It drummed on the roof as the chickens began to utter their medium alarm call, 'Bk-bk-bk, b'kak!'

Still Floridius slept on. His chubby cheeks were unshaven and his unbleached tunic spotted with red wine stains. He must have drunk at least four goblets of spiced wine the night before.

'Bk-bk-bk, B'KAK!' protested a fluffy black hen named Aphrodite. She was the best dancer, for she could strut out a double loop, the symbol for one thousand: ∞. But she hated the rain on her silky feathers and now she grumpily flapped down from the table. The others started to follow her.

'YO, SATURNALIA!' shouted Threptus at the top of his lungs.

CRACK! At the same moment a dazzling bolt of lightning lit up the shack.

'Thunder!' cried Floridius. He stumbled out of bed, jostling the low bedside table and knocking over the hot poculum Threptus had spent half an hour preparing. 'Quickly! Fetch my thunder scroll! I must find out what it means!'

'Bk-bk-bk, B'KAK!' Aphrodite was drenched in warm, eggy wine, her fluffy black feathers soaked and matted. Felix the kitten appeared from under Floridius's bed.

'Me-oww!' he said, and began to lap up the milky mixture.

'Eheu!' said Threptus. 'Oh, no!'

All his preparations had been for nothing. The soggy hens were sheltering beneath the slick tabletop. The rain had made their jaunty felt caps bleed dye so that the three youngest hens – white pullets – were now stained pink, blue and green. The white silky hen named Candida was streaked with purple.

Threptus put on a brave smile. He did not want his master to see him unhappy. Without Floridius, he would still be an orphan beggar boy sleeping rough in the graveyard.

But Floridius did not notice Threptus's wobbly smile or the spilled drink or even the colourful chickens under the table. He was unrolling a tattered papyrus roll. It was a special Etruscan almanac that told him what thunder meant on any given day of the year.

'I must find out what today's thunder omen means!' he cried. 'It could be something terrible!'

SCROLL II

'WHAT DAY IS IT?' MUTTERED Floridius the Soothsayer as he searched his thunder scroll.

'The Saturnalia,' said Threptus in a small voice. 'Today is the first day of Saturnalia.'

'First day of the Saturnalia?' lisped Floridius. 'Oh, that's a relief! If it thunders today, that means small locusts in the spring but a good crop anyway.' He looked up at his apprentice and his smile faded. 'Threptus!' he cried. 'What's the matter?'

Threptus felt his lower lip quivering. 'Yo, Saturnalia!' he said bravely.

Floridius dropped the thunder scroll onto the bed. 'What's wrong, me little friend? Did the thunder frighten you? It's only "Small Locust Thunder".'

Threptus tried to keep his voice steady. 'I didn't have a Saturnalia gift for you, so I made you a hot poculum with the only egg and I've been training the chickens to do a special dance, but the rain has ruined everything.'

'You don't need to give me anything!' Floridius went to Threptus and slung a chubby arm around the boy's shoulders.

'But I wanted to thank you for taking me in and making me your apprentice.'

Thunder rumbled again and a sudden gust threw a few hissing drops of rain onto the little clay oven in the corner. Beneath the table the chickens clucked miserably.

'Bk-bk-bk-bk-bk!'

'You don't have to thank me,' said Floridius.

'What have I given you? A leaky shack full of damp chickens.' He gave Threptus's shoulders a squeeze. 'But all that's going to change. By the end of the week we'll have new tiles on our roof and a glass skylight to make things cosy and warm.'

'A glass skylight?' breathed Threptus. He knew such things were rare and expensive.

'Yes,' said Floridius, looking up at the rainy hole in the roof. 'A glass skylight that can be put in for winter and taken out in the summertime. Imbrex said he'll do our roof for only a hundred sesterces: tiles, glass and all. Won't it be good to have a nice cosy home?'

Threptus gave a shivering nod. 'But where will we get one hundred sesterces?'

'Sigilla!' lisped Floridius. He went to his bed and pulled out two baskets full of moulded clay figurines. 'We have fifty of these statuettes to sell. My pal Tongilianus let me have them for just fifty sesterces. He told me they fell off the back of an ox-cart. Ha, ha, ha!'

Threptus put his panpipes on a chair and took a jangly step to the baskets. One basket was full of identical naked bearded men, each holding what looked like one of Pistor's big almond pastries. The other basket contained figurines of a woman in a long stola.

'Who is the naked man?' asked Threptus, picking up one of the figurines. 'He looks angry.'

'That is Jupiter Fulminata,' said Floridius. 'King of the gods.'

'What's he holding? It looks like one of Pistor's almond pastries.'

'You and your almond pastries!' laughed Floridius. 'Fulminata means "thunderer". That is his thunderbolt.'

'Is that what a thunderbolt looks like? Fat in the middle and pointy at either end? And twisty?'

Floridius nodded. 'Thunderbolts are often twisty,' he said. 'And sometimes they have lightning and wings.'

Outside the shack, a real thunderclap split the morning. Threptus quickly put the Jupiter back in his basket.

Floridius laughed and ruffled his hair. 'Don't worry,' he said. 'It's only "Small Locust Thunder".'

'But it was on the left-hand side,' said Threptus. 'Isn't that unlucky?'

'That only counts if you're seeking a specific omen. When the thunder's everywhere it's the day that counts.'

Threptus didn't really understand, so he just nodded. He picked up one of the female figurines. 'Who is the lady?'

'That's no lady!' cried Floridius. 'That's Jupiter's wife! Ha, ha!' He glanced heavenward and whispered, 'Forgive me, O Juno.'

'What are they for?' asked Threptus.

'You put them in your lararium and worship them.' Floridius pointed at the special shelf they used as a shrine, with its statuettes of Bacchus, a Lar and a lucky snake. 'Or you buy them as gifts for your children to play with.' He took one of the Jupiters from the basket and presented it to Threptus. 'Happy Saturnalia!'

'For me to keep?' said Threptus. 'Thank you, mentor!' He examined his figurine. 'I like this Jupiter,' he said. 'He doesn't look as angry as the other ones.'

Floridius nodded. 'Here! Have a little Juno,

too. I can't sell this one as she has a little crack in her backside.'

Threptus giggled. 'Thank you, mentor.' He carefully put the clay figurines on his pillow, one either side of Felix the kitten, who had curled up there to sleep off his breakfast of milky spiced wine.

'They're not works of art,' said Floridius, 'but I reckon we can ask five sesterces for each. If we sell them all at a profit of four sesterces each then we'll have . . .' He counted on his fingers, crinkled his nose, then shrugged. 'Well, more than enough money for roof tiles and a skylight. So let's get started.'

'You mean we have to work today?' said Threptus.

'Only until we earn enough to pay for the skylight,' said Floridius. 'Then we can celebrate!' He picked up his light blue cloak from the bed and put it on. 'If I carry the Jupiters, can you get the Junos?'

'Yes, mentor.' Threptus took off his belled ankle-bangle and put on his olive-green paenula. Then he picked up the heavy basket of Juno figurines.

As Floridius shouldered open the front door, the sacred hens ran clucking from beneath the table.

'That's one good thing about the rain,' said Floridius, as they followed the chickens outside. 'It brings out worms.'

Threptus grinned. 'And our hens love worms more than anything,' he said.

Floridius's shack was built on a piece of waste ground abutting the Temple of Rome and Augustus. A reed fence kept the chickens in and the foxes out. Threptus carefully closed the gate behind him, waved goodbye to the sacred hens and ran across the boggy ground after his master.

They rounded the corner of the temple to find at least five hundred cheerful Ostians milling about in the open space of the forum. Many of them wore jaunty Saturnalia caps, bigger versions of the ones Threptus had made for the chickens. Instead of the toga, some highborn men wore a long tunic with a matching cape called a synthesis. Everybody wore their warmest cloaks. The lucky ones had fur-lined boots. Despite the cold, damp weather, all the citizens of Ostia had happy faces and bright eyes.

'Yo, Saturnalia!' some of the Ostians called out to Threptus and Floridius.

'Yo, Saturnalia!' they replied.

The colonnade of the money-changers had been taken over by colourful Saturnalia stalls selling candles, sweets, garlands and figurines.

Floridius and Threptus were just approaching their spot at the far end of the colonnade when their way was blocked by a man in a toga flanked by two soldiers, one with a broken nose and the other with the biggest, blackest eyebrows Threptus had ever seen.

'Bato!' cried Floridius happily. 'You must be the only citizen wearing a toga rather than a synthesis, ha, ha!' He put down his basket of Jupiters and beamed with pleasure. 'Yo, Saturnalia!'

'No Saturnalia,' said the grim young magistrate, 'for you. Aulus Probus Floridius, I am officially revoking your licence to sell amulets, charms and other goods.'

'What? But you just granted me that last month.'

'In addition, I am seizing those two baskets of statuettes, which were reported stolen three days ago.'

'But, but . . .'

'And, finally, I must ask you to give me your shoulder bag. I will keep it until the end of the festival, in case it contains other stolen goods.'

'But it's only got me amulets against evil. You know, me squashed blue eyes and suchlike.'

Bato gestured to the soldiers. Broken Nose tugged Floridius's satchel from his shoulder. Black Eyebrows lifted the two baskets.

'But, I didn't steal these statuettes!' cried Floridius. 'I bought them from Tongilianus. Paid fifty sesterces for the lot.'

'You'll have to settle that in court after the festival.'

'No! This is me busiest time of year!' cried Floridius as Bato turned to go. 'You'll ruin me! How will I look after the boy?'

But Bato and the soldiers were walking away.

Threptus and Floridius looked at each other in dismay.

Then Threptus had an idea.

'Mentor!' he said. 'What about the reward

Bato promised you if he ever got engaged to the priest's daughter?'

'Oh, me little friend, you're a genius!' cried Floridius and he set off after Bato at a run, his cloak flapping and his sandals slapping.

SCROLL III

'**B**ATO! WAIT!' CHUBBY FLORIDIUS clutched at Bato's toga.

The young magistrate turned, his pale brown eyes blazing.

'Unhand me!' he cried.

The soldiers took a clanking step forward.

'Forgive me, sir,' cried Floridius, holding up his hands, 'but what ever happened to my reward?'

'Reward?'

'For my predicting your marriage to Lucilia, the beautiful daughter of the Priest of Vulcan!'

Bato glanced at the soldiers, then took a step forward, his eyes angry and his voice low. 'I told you never to speak of it in public.'

'But you said if the marriage came off you would give me one hundred sesterces as a reward!'

'For you there will be no reward,' muttered Bato from between clenched teeth.

'No reward?

'Lucilia turned me down,' he hissed.

'I don't understand!' cried Floridius. 'It was all arranged. All parties were in favour.'

'All except the girl!' said Bato. 'She told her father that she would not marry me.'

'But why not?'

'She saw some crows flying to her left on the day her father first spoke of me. And she had a bad dream that morning.'

'If only she had agreed to meet you,' said Floridius, 'she would have seen that you are highborn and handsome, important and powerful.'

'She did meet me.' Bato's ears grew pink. 'She said I was a stut-stut-stuttering fool.'

Threptus and Floridius glanced at each other in amazement. Neither of them had ever heard Bato stutter before.

'What's she done to you?' cried Floridius. 'She's bewitched you!'

Bato shook his head. 'I will not hear a word against her,' he said, lifting his chin. 'Your prophecy was wrong and there will be no reward. If it wasn't bad luck to imprison people during the Saturnalia,' he continued, 'I'd have you thrown in the basilica cells this very moment and I'd leave you there until the law-courts re-open.'

He turned and stalked off, followed by the two soldiers.

This time Floridius did not protest but stood dumbfounded.

A happy crowd of revellers engulfed them.

'Yo, Saturnalia!' they cried. Some of them carried wineskins and one or two jangled tambourines. They all wore colourful freed-men's hats.

'Ecce! Look!' said a youth in a floppy pink cap and red cloak. 'It's the soothsayer who sold me my good-luck charm: a willy-on-a-thong! Yo, Saturnalia!' He hooked his arm through Floridius's and spun him in a twirl.

'I've got one, too!' laughed a man in a grass-green cap. 'A willy-on-a-thong!'

'I want one!' said a husky-voiced woman in a mustard-yellow synthesis. 'Sell me a willy-on-a-thong, soothsayer!'

They all began to sing, 'Willy-on-a-thong! Willy-on-a-thong!'

'I'm sorry,' whimpered Floridius. 'The magistrate just confiscated them.'

'Then let's try the market!' cried the woman. And the group of revellers jingled off towards the colonnade, still singing, 'Willy-on-a-thong!'

Floridius sat heavily on the steps of the temple and put his head in his hands.

'I don't understand it!' he said miserably. 'How could this have happened? Gamala, the girl's father, was all for the marriage. He approved of Bato. Since when does the daughter have a say in whom she marries? Dear Bacchus, help me!'

'YO, SATURNALIA!' bellowed Praeco the town crier from his plinth in the centre of the forum. 'EGRILIUS THE JUNIOR MAGISTRATE PRESENTS A COMEDY PLAY FOR YOUR ENJOYMENT. GATHER ONE, GATHER ALL!'

Floridius lifted his head. He had a strange gleam in his eye. He sometimes got the same look when he'd drunk too much spiced wine.

'What is it?' cried Threptus.

'The play!' cried Floridius. 'We must watch the play!'

'But master, we need money to eat!'

'Yes, I know! And the gods will speak to us through the play. They always do. The play is sacred,' he said. 'Stories make everything right. Come!' He took Threptus's hand and together they mounted the steps of the temple. People were already claiming places but Floridius found a free spot on the highest step with a good view of the forum.

Threptus was hungry and damp, and sitting on the hard marble step made him colder than before. Many of the people around him were gnawing glazed pork chops and spare ribs from the dawn sacrifice to the god Saturn. The roast meat smelled wonderful and Threptus's stomach growled. He pressed it to keep it quiet, but this made it rumble even louder.

'Shhh!' said Floridius, pointing. 'Look. Listen. Learn.'

In the forum below them, a tubby man was mounting the steps of a makeshift platform. Dressed in an apricot-coloured tunic and leggings, he tottered on high platform shoes and wore a mask with a great, gaping frozen grin. Those masks always made Threptus smile and shudder at the same time.

'Crepitus!' screeched a woman. 'Crepitus the Thunderer!'

Threptus tugged his master's cloak. 'Isn't "crepitus" a rude word?' he asked.

'Yes,' giggled Floridius. 'Shouldn't use it in polite conversation. But during the Saturnalia, anything is allowed!'

Around them, people started chanting, 'Crepitus the Thunderer! Crepitus the Thunderer!'

Down on the stage, Crepitus bowed and addressed the crowd.

'Yo, Saturnalia!' he cried. The gaping grin of a mouth in his mask seemed to magnify his words.

'Yo, Saturnalia!' everybody responded.

'Senators, Patricians, Equestrians, Plebs and Slaves!' proclaimed the actor. 'Welcome to our humble Saturnalia farce. Today we present a play entitled "The Divorce", a musical comedy in three acts. My name is Crepitus and I play the part of Bucco the Babbler! I can speak from both ends!' With this he turned his back to the audience, bent over and emitted a textured burp from his large and wobbly bottom. It was the loudest, longest, rudest crepitus Threptus had ever heard.

'That's why they call him "the Thunderer",' giggled Floridius. 'And *that* kind of thunder is a good omen because it keeps away evil.'

Threptus stared at his master in dismay. Everything had been taken from them, and now he was laughing at an actor whose main talent was breaking wind. Had Floridius gone mad?

SCROLL IV

T HREPTUS AND FLORIDIUS SAT
watching the rude Saturnalia farce.

Crepitus the Thunderer played Bucco the
Babbler. The other three members of his troupe
played Maccus the Fool, Dossennus the Glutton
and Pappus the Old Man. Each of the four
main characters wore a different coloured tunic
and a brightly painted mask. The masks had

exaggerated features and gaping mouths that projected the actors' voices right into Threptus's ears.

As they watched, Floridius explained that each of these characters had a special weakness or flaw. Bucco was crafty, Maccus was lazy, Dossennus was greedy and Pappus tried to kiss women too young for him.

'Each one's flaw is his downfall,' said Floridius. 'We laugh at them because they are like us.'

Threptus stared at his master; was *his* flaw that he was *crazy*?

'Watch and listen,' said Floridius, the fevered gleam still in his eye. 'The gods will give us an answer!'

On the stage the four actors were dancing in unison and emitting rude noises each time they kicked up their legs. Threptus could not understand how four windy men in masks and platform shoes could have the answer to anything.

But the crowd adored it. The people around him were rolling on the temple steps and a grey-haired lady in lavender was crying with laughter.

Presently the old man named Pappus told

the audience how he was trying to make a pretty young maid fall in love with him. He had given her a love salad of white radishes, which everyone knew fired the passions. 'But my wife ate it,' he told the audience. 'And the side effects were frightening.'

He turned his back on the audience and imitated Crepitus by breaking wind.

The audience roared with laughter.

A new character strutted onto the stage. It was a man in a towering wig and a turquoise stola. It was Crepitus, playing the part of a woman.

'I am Pappa's wife,' he said to the audience in a high voice. 'You may call me Flatula!'

Everyone loved this.

'I will not stay married to that dirty old man!' Flatula proclaimed. 'There was a time when we used to like watching the sunset together and singing duets. But now we have nothing in common! I want a divorce.'

Flatula gave one of the loudest bottom-burps yet. It caused three pigeons to fly up from a basket opened by Dossennus the Glutton, who thought he had bought oven-ready birds.

'The omens are good for the divorce!'

Dossennus said to Flatula. 'My dinner flew up on the right side of old granddad.'

The crowd laughed and applauded. But Floridius leapt to his feet.

'Eureka!' he cried.

'What is it, mentor?' asked Threptus.

'Sit down!' cried some people behind them.

Floridius sat down. 'I have the answer to our problems!' he cried. 'The play just showed me how to get Lucilia to change her mind and marry Bato!'

'Shhh!' said some people around them. The grey-haired lady in the lavender stola was giving them a strange look.

'How?' whispered Threptus.

'Guess!' whispered Floridius. 'It was something in the play. Guess how we will convince her to marry Bato.'

'By giving her a love salad made of white radishes?' said Threptus in his mentor's ear.

'Good guess, but no. That only gives you wind,' giggled Floridius.

'By finding something they like doing together? Like watching the sunset or playing duets?'

'Good guess, but no. Remember what Bato said? How she's easily influenced by omens?'

'By getting our sacred chickens to fly up on the right?'

'Good guess,' whispered Floridius, 'but chickens don't really fly.' He paused and then said, 'But what *do* they do?'

'They eat!' cried Threptus. 'If our sacred chickens eat then the omens are good!'

'Exactly! All we have to do is take the sacred chickens to Lucilia and ask them to eat if the omens are good for her to marry Bato!'

'Shhh!' said some people on the steps nearby.

'And our chickens are always hungry,' whispered Threptus, 'so they always eat.'

'That,' hissed Floridius, 'is the beauty of my plan! See,' he lisped. 'I told you the gods would speak through the play. Come on!'

'Where are we going?'

'To make an appointment to read the omens for Lucilia and her father as soon as possible!'

At last, it seemed as if the gods were smiling on them.

They found Gamala at home, and he invited

them to come and read the omens in his daughter's presence the very next morning.

They found Imbrex in the Forum of Corporations and Floridius told him to deliver the roof tiles as soon as possible.

Finally, they used Floridius's last sestertius to buy two thunderbolt-shaped almond pastries from Pistor's son, Porcius, who was manning a stall in the colonnade. He told them he did not mind working on the Saturnalia because he got to keep all the profits. The thunder-pastries were delicious: honey-sweet and chewy with almond flakes.

But when Threptus and Floridius got back to their shack, happy and sticky, they made a terrible discovery.

SCROLL V

'WHAT'S HAPPENED TO OUR POOR hens?' cried Floridius, as they stepped through the front door.

All eighteen chickens had gone into the shack via a small chicken hole in the wall. Now they covered the floor, each and every one of them too bloated to move.

'Look!' cried Threptus, pointing to the empty

bag of pearl barley on the floor. 'Someone knocked it off the shelf and the chickens ate it all up!'

The eight dancing chickens still wore their conical felt Saturnalia hats. They looked like miniature Saturnalia revellers who had feasted and drunk all day long.

'Eheu!' said Floridius. 'Who could have done this?'

'Meee-ow!' said Felix the kitten. He emerged from under the table where he had been curled up between two hens.

'Bad kitty!' scolded Floridius.

Threptus picked up Felix and stroked his soft fur. 'He didn't mean to,' said Threptus. 'He was probably just exploring and knocked over the sack so that the barley spilled out everywhere. It was my fault,' he said. 'I forgot to tie it up.'

'But don't you see?' said Floridius. 'I never feed chickens the day before they have to prophesy.'

'Oh!' cried Threptus. 'I forgot about that. Maybe they'll be hungry tomorrow?'

'Look at them!' cried Floridius. 'They look like balls made of feathers. They won't be hungry for days. How can we convince Gamala's daughter to marry Bato if they won't eat?'

'Aphrodite might not be able to eat,' said Threptus, 'but she can still make the symbol for one thousand which looks like the letter B. Aphrodite! Where are you?'

An answering 'Bk!' came from beneath the table. There she was, still matted from the poculum but now as bloated as the others. 'Bk!' she repeated miserably.

'We can't take her to Gamala's looking like that!' cried Floridius. 'I don't think a sorry-looking chicken describing a B will convince the priest's daughter to marry Bato.'

When he saw the expression on Threptus's face, he patted his head. 'Don't feel bad, me little friend. Let's get them back in their coop where they can't do themselves any more harm.'

They tried to shoo the hens out into the yard but most were too bloated to move. Only the three formerly white pullets and white-and-purple Candida were able to waddle outdoors and up the ramp of the henhouse. Floridius and Threptus had to carry the rest.

'I just hope they're all right,' said Floridius, when he had shut the chickens in. He sat dejectedly on the board ramp.

Threptus patted his master's shoulder. He hated to see him looking so sad. The inner ends of Floridius's eyebrows went up and the corners of his mouth went down, so that his face looked like the mask of a tragic actor.

That gave Threptus an idea.

'Let's go and watch another play in the forum,' he suggested.

Floridius perked up. 'That's a good idea,' he said. Then he slumped down. 'Only the next farce isn't until tomorrow morning.' Then he sat up straight again. 'But there might be a pantomime in the theatre, and they usually start around noon. I haven't been to one in ages,' he said. 'I'm usually too busy selling my wares in the forum.'

'A pantomime in the *theatre*?' Threptus swallowed hard.

'Of course,' said Floridius, standing up. 'You've been before, haven't you?'

Threptus shook his head.

'You've never been to the theatre? Then come on!'

Threptus followed his mentor reluctantly out through the reed gate. He had never told his master, but the theatre was the one place in Ostia he was afraid to go.

SCROLL VI

F ROM THE OUTSIDE, OSTIA'S THEATRE
looked like a giant red brick cake that some
god had cut in half. Rising four stories high, it
was pierced with arches at the lower three levels
and topped with masts for a big canvas awning
to keep off the rain.

It was so tall that from the ground the masts
looked like toothpicks. Threptus felt dizzy just

looking at it. The thought of going inside made him queasy. Floridius wanted them to go into the theatre's main entrance because he had a token. But Threptus hesitated. The dim vaulted tunnel looked like the throat of a beast that wanted to devour him.

The town bully Naso had often warned Threptus and the other beggar boys that the theatre was a dangerous place. There were hundreds of passageways, but most of them were dead ends, he said, patrolled by soldiers waiting to arrest orphans in order to sell them to slave-dealers. Naso had also told them about a horrible room called a vomitorium where wealthy Romans went to vomit up their dinner to make space for more.

Threptus was almost certain that a vomitorium was just a fancy word for 'exit' or 'entrance' and that soldiers probably didn't arrest orphans. But why would Naso warn them about the theatre if there was no danger? It had always been a mystery to Threptus and the other beggars.

Threptus wanted to follow Floridius into the vomitorium of the theatre, but his legs refused to move.

A thought popped into Threptus's head. 'What would Lupus do?'

Lupus was Threptus's hero: an eight-year-old beggar-boy who had become a rich ship-owner by the time he was ten. Lupus was legendary among the other beggar-boys for his bravery in solving mysteries and facing fierce opponents.

Don't be afraid. Go in! Lupus seemed to be saying in his right ear.

If you go in there, the soldiers will get you! Naso seemed to be saying in his left ear.

Threptus took a deep breath, made the sign against evil and followed his mentor through the arched entrance into a dim vaulted tunnel.

He looked around, in case any soldiers were on the lookout for orphaned beggar boys. But among the happy crowd he did not see any soldiers. Then he looked down for traces of slimy sick on the ground. Nothing. That proved Naso had lied: a vomitorium was just an entrance to the theatre.

A moment later he emerged into the bright, airy theatre. Threptus looked around in wonder.

If the outside of the theatre was half a red

brick cake, the inside was like half a giant marble bowl. The bowl was made of bands of curved stone steps rising up almost to the top and divided into wedges by aisles.

The seats faced a long marble stage, and behind this stage was a luxury apartment building about a hundred feet high.

Threptus gawped. A lofty apartment building in a theatre?

Then he gasped as someone grasped a fistful of his cloak.

'Come on, me little friend,' wheezed Floridius. 'I thought I'd lost you!'

Threptus pointed at the hundred-foot-tall apartment building with its doors, windows and columns. 'Is that where the actors live?'

'That's the scaena,' lisped Floridius. 'It's the backdrop of the stage. There's nothing behind that. It's a flat wooden façade, painted to look like marble.' He pointed to the stage. 'That's the scaenae frons and this half circle we're standing on is the orchestra. And that,' he turned and gestured to the three curved bands of seats rising up, 'is called the cavea because it's hollow like a cave.' He bent his head and whispered, 'You can see we get a posher sort of crowd in the theatre, even though it's free and anyone can come. Magistrates, senators and priests get proper chairs on low steps near the front. See?'

Threptus nodded. 'Where do we sit?' he asked.

Floridius grinned. 'We, my boy, are plebs. So we should go to the highest band of seats . . .' he opened his hand to reveal a small bone coin, '. . . unless we have a ticket!'

'Is that a ticket?' Threptus took the disc. 'I thought you said the theatre was free.'

'It is, but posh people get these so they can sit in the best seats. I bought this one off an old Etruscan. Only five sesterces. Look. "CAV I" means we are in the first cavea or band of seating. "CVN II" means we're in the middle wedge of seats. And "GRAD VII" means we're seven seats up,' he said.

They found a place on the seventh row in the second wedge between a fat patrician and the priest of Hercules. Threptus looked around at all the people now filling every seat. The lady in lavender was in the next row down, and two rows behind he saw a rich perfume-maker's widow called Allia Porra and her slave-girl. But they had traded clothes and Allia held a parasol over Zmyrna's head!

'Yo, Saturnalia!' A familiar voice from the stage brought Threptus's head round.

'Yo, Saturnalia!' replied three thousand Ostians.

'It's Bato!' cried Threptus.

'So it is!' said Floridius, his eyes wide. 'He must be the sponsor.'

'What is a "sponsor"?' asked Threptus.

'It means he pays the troupe to perform. That's why it's free!'

'Last year,' proclaimed Bato, 'when I was running for the position of duumvir I promised you plays and theatre. I am duly sponsoring a different pantomime every afternoon for the next five days of this great festival . . .' His voice was drowned out by cheers and applause.

He gave a little bow. 'Today,' he continued, 'I am proud to present the finest pantomime dancer of our day, fresh from a tour of North Africa. Please welcome Narcissus and his troupe!'

As Bato exited stage left, four musicians ran out into the orchestra at the foot of the stage. The people were clapping with cupped hands. It made a strange hollow sound.

'Why are they clapping like that?' Threptus asked.

'It's called "roof tiles",' said Floridius. 'It's made by clapping with your hands curved like tiles. Normal clapping with flat hands is called "bricks" because bricks are flat. "Roof tiles" are the highest praise an audience can give. Apart from throwing coins and jewels,' he added.

Threptus tried clapping with his hands curved like tiles and got the knack just as everyone else fell silent. He was the only one clapping! He glanced around in case his ignorance had attracted a soldier's attention, but nobody was looking at him. Everyone was staring at the stage, so he did too.

The pantomime dancer had appeared there as if by magic. He wore tight flesh-coloured leggings under a knee-length red tunic with a little cape and a floppy Persian hat on his head. On his face was a mask. Unlike the masks of the comic actors, his had a closed mouth. He stood waiting, looking out at the audience . . . looking straight out at Threptus!

The musicians began to play, and he began to move.

The frizzy-haired female singer chanted the prelude to the story of Anchises, a handsome young shepherd of Troy who was loved by Venus, the beautiful goddess of love.

Threptus lost track of time. He was transported to faraway mountains by the words and music, and by Narcissus the dancer in the role of Anchises.

Anchises rescued a lamb and drank from the stream and ate an apple. Each gesture was so perfectly mimed that Threptus could almost feel the lamb, hear the stream and taste the apple.

When Anchises pretended to take off his clothes to bathe in the stream, some of the girls in the audience squealed, 'Narcissus!' but their neighbours shushed them. Then everyone laughed as Anchises stopped mid-scrub to look up, sensing that he was being spied upon. They knew from the singer's narration that Venus, the goddess of love, was watching the handsome shepherd from on high!

The audience grew quiet again as one of the musicians produced the burbling trill of a bird with a water-filled clay whistle. It heralded the arrival of beautiful Venus, dressed as a shepherdess. The audience could not see her but when Anchises went to her, they seemed to embrace! It took Threptus a moment to realise that Narcissus was hugging himself.

The whole theatre held its breath as Anchises and the invisible goddess sank to the ground. The singer's clear voice told how Anchises and Venus lay together and how the next morning she sternly warned him not to tell anyone about their night of passion. With a farewell kiss and a vow, he promised it would always be their secret.

Hardly had Anchises waved Venus out of sight when unheard voices made him turn. Some of his friends had just arrived. They teased him for being a humble shepherd with no excitement in his life. Little did he know that someone was watching him from on high.

A murmur of excitement ran round the theatre and Floridius nudged Threptus. 'Look up there,' he whispered. 'It's Venus!'

On the very top of the backdrop, Threptus saw a slim-hipped, big-busted woman in a turquoise stola, wearing a Venus mask. It made Threptus dizzy to see someone up so high without a rail.

'Don't tell your friends about Venus!' screeched a woman in the audience. 'She's watching you!'

Anchises did not hear the warning. He boasted to his friends, 'I spent the night with Venus herself!'

Suddenly a deafening rumble made everyone in the theatre jump! Jupiter had thundered!

SCROLL VII

'WAS THAT REAL THUNDER?' THREPTUS asked Floridius.

Without taking his eyes from the pantomime dancer, Floridius shook his head and pointed towards the musicians. On a wooden frame near the stage hung a rectangular sheet of bronze about half the height of a man. The round-faced musician was stroking it slowly with a wooden mallet to make it rumble. As Threptus watched, he struck it hard to make a resounding thunderclap.

On the stage, Anchises froze. He had heard the thunder, too.

Suddenly the crowd gasped.

'Look!' whispered Floridius, pointing.

Venus had disappeared and another figure stood on top of the backdrop, on the unlucky left. Like Venus, this figure was slim and wearing turquoise. But it had no breasts and the mask showed it was Jupiter: angry Jupiter! The god lifted up a bright golden object. It looked like one of Pistor's twisty almond pastries but it was the size of a sword.

Threptus's eyes grew wide. He knew what that was!

'A thunderbolt!' sang the singer. 'Jupiter Fulminata was furious when Venus told him that Anchises had broken his vows of silence!'

Poised like a lofty tightrope walker, Jupiter held the thunderbolt aloft for a few dramatic moments. Then he threw it down. It struck the ground near Anchises with a massive crack and a puff of smoke. When the smoke cleared, Anchises was lying on the ground.

All over the theatre women screamed, and a girl three rows down from Threptus fainted.

The music was low and sober as Anchises slowly regained consciousness . . . to find he was blind! And when he tried to rise to his feet he discovered that one of his legs had been twisted by the bolt.

'Oh! *The fierce, pure, awful anger of the goddess Venus,'* sang the singer.

All over the theatre Threptus heard the soft sound of stifled sobs. His own eyes were brimming. Anchises looked so pathetic as he limped painfully across the stage, blindly groping with his hands. Threptus stole a glance at his master and saw that Floridius was sobbing silently, his chubby face wet and pink.

On stage, Anchises groped his way to one of the doors in the scaena, gave a single backward look, and disappeared. A few moments later another figure appeared from the central double doors. This figure seemed to be an old nursemaid, cradling a baby. She had no Persian hat and wore a different mask, but Threptus recognised the flesh-coloured leggings beneath her blue stola. A quick costume change meant Narcissus was playing this part, too!

Down in the orchestra, the singer sang of a bittersweet ending: nine months later Venus gave birth to a little boy. That little boy was named Aeneas. He would be a great warrior, and one day he would carry his lame old father, Anchises, out of burning Troy. Aeneas, son of Anchises, would sail to found a new nation, the greatest nation of all: Rome!

The old nursemaid held up Baby Aeneas as the singer sang: *'You are the descendents of Venus and Anchises! You have the divine in you, but also the proud and foolish braggart! Take care, O Roman, to draw upon your divine half!'*

Then the old nursemaid bowed and removed her mask to reveal the face of Narcissus, handsome beneath a sheen of sweat.

The crowd erupted into thunderous applause. They were giving him 'bricks' and 'roof tiles' and screaming their approval. Threptus found himself lifted to his feet by a strange emotion he had never felt before. He was just an ex-beggar boy, with an absent mother and a father whose name he did not know, but he was a Roman! He was descended from Aeneas, son of Anchises and Venus!

He felt drained and yet full. His legs were wobbly and his heart was beating hard and his eyes prickled with tears.

All the exits of the theatre meant that it was emptying quickly. As he and Floridius filed out among other happy and orderly Ostians, Threptus had a sudden urge to hug every one of them. They had all laughed and gasped and cried together. They were his family. He did not need a father or a mother, for all these people were his aunts and uncles and grandparents. And especially dear, chubby, unshaven Floridius, who looked after him as best he could.

If only he could help his master arrange the marriage of Bato and Lucilia, and get the reward.

Threptus saw one of the musicians opening a door of the scaena so that the other two could put the thunder-sheet away. At that moment, an idea popped into Threptus's head like a bolt from Jupiter.

It was an idea so brilliant that he stopped dead

in his tracks and someone bumped into him. He turned to see the grey-haired lady in her lavender stola and palla.

'Excuse me, domina,' said Threptus politely. Then he ran to catch up with Floridius. 'Eureka!' he cried. 'I have the answer!'

'What?'

'The story gave me the answer, just like you said!' Threptus beckoned Floridius down to his level and whispered the brilliant idea into his ear.

He watched as a huge smile spread across his mentor's face. 'Threptus,' he proclaimed. 'You are a genius!'

SCROLL VIII

T HE SECOND DAY OF THE SATURNALIA dawned clear and bright, but very cold. Threptus woke up shivering.

Inside the shack the coals in the small clay oven were cool and there was frost on the table. Outside, there was a skin of ice over the water in the rain barrel. Threptus longed for the day their little house would be warm and cosy. If only they could convince the priest's daughter Lucilia to marry Bato. If only he would give them their promised reward. Then they could tile the roof and plug up the compluvium with a thick square of pale green glass.

Threptus tried to find a live coal to revive the fire while Floridius went to see how the sacred chickens were doing.

His mentor came back a short time later with Candida under one arm. The fluffy white hen was still as round as a ball and streaked with purple.

'She and the pullets are the only ones who greeted me,' he said. 'They're young and she's lowest on the pecking order so I think she got a little less food than the others. Let's see if she'll eat.' He sprinkled a few grains of barley on the floor.

Candida did not utter a peep nor did she eat. She sat where she was.

'Oh dear,' said Floridius and scratched his head. 'We have to bring at least one chicken this morning. But it's no good if she just sits there like a fluffy ball.'

Threptus stroked Candida's white and purple feathers. They were as silky as the fur of his kitten Felix, but even puffier. She was a beautiful hen.

'I know how to get her moving,' he said through chattering teeth. He handed his mentor the panpipes he had made from river reeds. 'Here, blow on these. She should walk in a circle. It's the chicken dance I spent the last two weeks training them to do.'

Floridius looked doubtful, but when he blew on the pipes Candida heaved herself up and began to move.

'Look, master!' cried Threptus excitedly. 'She's doing a double loop, like Aphrodite! We can get her to do B for Bato.'

'Euge!' cried Floridius, 'Praise the gods. Now, are you sure you're willing to climb up the vine again and open the double doors of Gamala's study?'

Threptus shivered with fear as well as cold. But he seemed to hear Lupus saying, *'Be brave. Be brave!'* so he nodded. 'Yes, mentor. I'm ready.'

It was too early for most people to be out. As they made their way to Gamala's house, they saw only a few bleary-eyed revellers who had not yet gone to bed. Threptus carried Candida, and Floridius had a large flat rectangular object in a burlap carrying sack.

On this frosty morning, the alley near the Laurentum Gate was deserted. There wasn't even washing on the clothesline of the apartment house next door.

Threptus blew on his frozen fingers to warm them, then glanced right and left. They seemed to be alone.

Floridius nodded and gave Threptus a thumbs-up.

Threptus put down Candida and started up the vine. When he was nearly at the window he stopped and looked down. Floridius was holding up the burlap sack. Threptus reached down and caught the cord at the top of the thunder-sheet and pulled it up and out of its sack. The sheet of bronze was almost as big as he was, thin but heavy. Would the vine hold them both? Carefully, he climbed higher, holding the softly grumbling thunder-sheet in his left hand. When he reached the small square window, he peeped in. Gamala's scroll room was empty and dark. Threptus struggled a little higher and slid his right leg in the window. Then, straddling the bottom of the window, partly in and partly out, he hooked the cord at the top of the thunder-sheet over a twig sticking out of the vine. The thunder-sheet was too big to push through the little window, but he hoped it would still sound impressive when he banged it.

Would the vine hold it?

Yes.

He looked down and saw Floridius give him a thumbs-up. Threptus's heart was pounding but he thought of brave Lupus and let himself in with hardly a sound. For a moment he sat in the study, letting the swooshing of blood in his ears get quieter. From both inside and outside he could hear Floridius knocking on the door downstairs. He looked around the small room with its scroll-covered walls, then he crawled to the double doors and put his ear to the crack between them. He could just make out the sound of Lucilia's little lap dog yapping and Floridius saying. 'I don't mind! He's jumping up on the lucky right side. But you'll need to put him in another room before the sacred chicken does her dance.'

The excited barking of the dog grew muffled and the voice of Floridius grew louder.

'Yes,' said Floridius. 'This little courtyard is perfect. If the gods want to send us a sign we will easily see it. Come, let us face north.'

That was Threptus's signal to open the double doors.

'That's a very strange-looking chicken,' came a female voice. 'Why does he have purple streaks?'

'Candida,' said Floridius, easy to hear now the doors were open, 'is my most exotic chicken. She is also the best at predicting marriages. If we are very lucky she will write the first letter of your ideal groom's name.'

'Are her feathers supposed to look like that?'

'Yes, of course. Hmmm. Ummm. Bummm.'

Threptus could not resist having a peek at the beautiful Lucilia. He got down on his tummy and wormed his way across the inner walkway to the safety rail. Peering down between the rails, he could see Floridius with his hands up, as if in prayer, intoning his babble to the gods. Candida the hen sat at his feet, quiet and subdued. A girl moved out from beneath the shelter of the peristyle. Threptus could see that her glossy brown hair was pinned up with pearl-headed pins and that she wore a fringed stola of fine pink wool.

Floridius's face was turned to the heavens and when he opened his eyes he saw Threptus peering down at him. He frowned and pushed the palms of his hands forward, as if telling Threptus to get back out of sight. 'Hmmm. Ummm. Bummm,' he warned.

Threptus obediently scooted back. He could not see, but at least he could hear.

'Oh Jupiter, Juno, Minerva,' intoned Floridius, 'and especially you, O Venus – Oh and you, too, Vulcan, whose high priest dwells here in this house – help to show us whom this young woman should marry.' Threptus heard the breathy sound of the panpipes and smiled to himself.

'Isn't she going to eat?' said Lucilia. 'I thought the sacred chickens ate.'

The panpipes broke off.

'Any chicken can eat,' said Floridius. 'Your

father will tell you that. But look! This chicken is dancing. If the gods decree, she will spell out the first letter of your beloved's name.'

'Really?'

'Really.'

The panpipes sounded again.

'She looks drunk,' said Lucilia doubtfully.

The music stopped and Floridius said, 'Look carefully. I think you'll find she's describing the letter B for Bato.'

'Oh, she is! She is!' Threptus heard the sound of hands clapping. 'Pater, look at that!' And then, less happily, 'Do you really think the gods want me to marry Bato?'

'Yes, my dear. I do,' Lucilia's father replied.

Floridius prayed again, 'Oh Jupiter, Juno, Minerva, and especially you, O Venus – Oh and you, too, Vulcan . . . we see the sacred chicken spelling out a B for Bato. If it is really your will for Lucilia to marry him, give us a sign. Especially you, O Jupiter . . .'

This was Threptus's cue!

He took the wooden mallet out of the

front of his tunic and scampered back to the window.

The previous afternoon Floridius had traded his own willy-on-a-thong amulet to the musician named Hanno in Narcissus's troop. In return they had been given permission to borrow the thunder-sheet and wooden mallet until noon the following day.

From the courtyard below, Floridius cried, 'Come, O Jupiter, give us a sign!'

Threptus reached his hand out of the window and stroked the bronze sheet with the mallet, the way Hanno had the day before. In the narrow space of the brick-faced alley the bronze rumbled loudly.

'Thunder!' cried Floridius. 'I believe I hear thunder from the right . . .'

Suddenly the sheet of bronze slipped from its twig and fell crashing to the cobblestones below. Threptus clapped his hands to his cheeks in horror. The deafening crash sounded like the most terrifying thunderclap he had ever heard.

As the sound of the bronze thunder faded, Threptus heard Lucilia scream.

'I'm going to die!' she screamed. 'I'm going to die!'

And she only stopped screaming when she fainted.

SCROLL IX

'IT'S MY OWN FAULT,' SAID FLORIDIUS AS they were trudging home with the thunder-sheet safely back in its burlap bag. 'I forgot that Lucilia was so superstitious. I of all people should have known not to do the reading this morning.'

'Why?' asked Threptus, who held Candida the silky white hen in his arms.

Floridius pointed up to the pure blue sky above. 'Thunder from a clear sky is a terrible omen,' he said.

'I'm sorry,' said Threptus. 'I thought it would be a good idea.'

'It is a good idea, me little friend. It was just unlucky that this was the first clear morning we've had all week. I should have rescheduled.'

'Lucilia won't really die will she?'

''Course she won't. But I might, if Bato ever finds out what we did.'

Threptus hung his head and stroked Candida sadly. She had described a clear letter B and had almost changed Lucilia's mind. Then the thunder had ruined everything.

'At least we got away without Gamala discovering our trick,' said Floridius. 'It was quick-thinking on your part to go down the vine, grab the thunder-sheet and hide round the corner.'

Threptus said nothing. He knew his mentor was only trying to cheer him.

'We'd better go straight to the theatre as soon as we drop off Candida,' continued Floridius.

'I promised Hanno I'd get the thunder-sheet back by noon. I need one of the gods to tell me what to do next. Eheu!' he cried. 'I forgot Imbrex!'

They had just emerged onto the waste ground leading to their shack. A burly man stood outside the reed fence. He held the lead of a skinny mule hitched to a two-wheeled cart full of orangey-red terracotta roof tiles.

'Imbrex!' said Floridius, putting on a cheerful voice. 'Yo, Saturnalia! What are you doing here?' Floridius leaned the sacked thunder-sheet against the fence and took Candida from Threptus.

'Yo!' grunted Imbrex. 'I'm just delivering the roof tiles you ordered.'

'What? So soon?' Floridius laughed nervously as he dropped Candida over the fence and into the chicken run.

'I need my hundred sesterces.'

'Right now?' cried Floridius. 'Can't I pay you next week?'

'That was not the deal,' said Imbrex. 'We agreed that I would tile your roof and fit the

73

skylight for a hundred sesterces, but only if you paid me by Saturnalia.'

'But . . . I don't have the cash,' said Floridius. 'I've had a streak of bad luck. As soon as the bankers go back to work I can borrow—'

'You ordered these tiles,' growled Imbrex, 'and by Hercules, you'll have them!' He tipped a lever and the whole load of tiles slid down onto the soggy ground.

'No!' cried Floridius. 'Take them back.'

'Pay me in the next three days,' said Imbrex, waving a forefinger, 'or I'll summon you to the law-courts!'

'No,' said another voice. '*I'll* summon him to the law-courts!'

'Tongilianus!' said Floridius as a small man in a grubby tunic limped up from the direction of the forum.

'Why did you tell the magistrate you got those statuettes from me? Now I'm in trouble! I'll take you to law-court and prove I didn't sell them to you.'

'But you *did* sell them to me.'

'You two will have to wait your turn!' cried

a third voice. '*I'm* taking this scoundrel to law-court first!'

Marcus Artorius Bato and his two soldiers were striding towards them. The magistrate's face was white with anger.

'Floridius!' he cried. 'I have just had a visit from the Priest of Vulcan. He tells me his daughter has taken to her bed and is dying of fright following a visit from you. What happened?'

'Nothing, sir!' Floridius gave a sheepish smile. 'I was just trying to convince her to marry you, that's all!'

'Grab him!' Bato commanded the guards. 'Throw him in the law-court cells!'

'But it's the Saturnalia!' protested Floridius. 'It's bad luck to imprison people during the festival.'

'My luck can't get any worse,' said Bato through gritted teeth.

'Wait!' cried Threptus bravely, as the soldiers seized Floridius. 'That's not fair. It was my fault.'

'Very well,' said Bato. 'Arrest the boy, as well.'

The two soldiers had each grasped one of

Floridius's arms. They looked at each other. Threptus knew they were wondering which of them should let go and grab him.

'Run, Threptus! Run!' cried Floridius.

Threptus ran.

A moment later he heard the clink of armour as one of the soldiers started after him. But he had a good head start, and he was small and fast. It was easy for Threptus to elude the pursuing soldier. He charged up one side-street and down another, then squeezed through a passageway near the Forum Baths. This route was one he and his beggar friends had often used, because it was too narrow for adults to pass through. Finally he raced down Orchard Street and out through the Laurentum Gate.

Once safely in the necropolis, he found one of his old hiding-places and sat panting and grinning with relief. But his smile soon faded and he began to despair. He was sheltering in a dank tomb in the graveyard, just like in his begging days. But this time he had no friends with him. He was alone and cold and hungry. His master was in prison and it was his fault.

Fresh storm clouds were gathering and one of them blotted out the sun. The midwinter noon seemed more like midnight.

He had to do something.

But what? What would Lupus do?

For once he had no idea.

HIDING IN A TOMB OUTSIDE OSTIA'S town wall Threptus prayed 'Please, one of you gods . . . Help me?'

Outside it had started to rain and Jupiter thundered.

It was real thunder, not fake. Was it an omen? Or was Jupiter just angry?

A thought made Threptus bang his head on

the low roof of the tomb. The thunder-sheet! He had to return it before the next pantomime or someone else would be summoning his master to court.

Cautiously, he made his way back home via backstreets and alleys. Bato and the soldiers had long gone, and he was not important enough for them to post a guard.

The thunder-sheet was still in the burlap bag, leaning up against the reed fence where Floridius had put it. Threptus breathed a sigh of relief.

He shouldered the heavy bag and made his way to the theatre. The Decumanus Maximus was becoming crowded as people made their way to the second pantomime of the Saturnalia.

Threptus kept his hood up and his head down as he shuffled along with the rest of the crowd through the main vomitorium.

Once inside the bright vast bowl of the theatre, he felt a gleam of hope. Surely everything was possible here. Didn't Floridius always say stories made everything right? He glanced around to make sure no soldiers were watching, then went up five marble stairs to the stage and opened the first door he came to. It was a dim storage room full of musical instruments. And there was the frame for the thunder-sheet. He put down the burlap bag and pulled out the bronze sheet and stood on tiptoe to hang it on its stand.

As he turned to go, he yelped with terror.

For there stood Jupiter, his glaring mask on his face and a thunderbolt in his hand.

'Oi!' said Jupiter. 'What you doing with my thunder?'

Threptus backed away from the thunder-sheet and groped behind him for the door handle.

He knew it was just a person in platform shoes wearing a Jupiter mask, but in the small, dim room the figure seemed real and frightening.

'I asked what you was doing,' said the loud but strangely familiar voice. 'You ain't supposed to be back here.'

Threptus stopped groping for the door handle. 'Naso?' he said. 'Is that you?'

Naso was Threptus's worst enemy. He had turned from begging to stealing, and resented the fact that Threptus preferred honest work to being a member of his gang.

'Yeah, it's me,' Naso removed the Jupiter mask and hung it on a peg. 'What you doing back here?'

'One of the musicians let us borrow his thunder,' stammered Threptus. 'I was just returning it.'

Naso tottered forward on his platform shoes and grabbed a handful of Threptus's tunic. 'Didn't I tell you lot never to come to the theatre? Didn't I warn you about the soldiers and the vomit and all?'

Threptus was too frightened to speak so he merely nodded.

'Don't you tell no-one,' he growled. 'Or I'll thump you. Understand?'

'I promise not to tell,' squeaked Threptus, and added, 'You're very brave.'

'Brave?'

'To stand a hundred feet high without a rail or anything,' Threptus took a deep breath and added, 'I think the boys would be proud of you.'

Naso let go of Threptus with a flourish of bravado. 'Nah. Can't let the boys know I got a proper job. So don't you tell no-one!'

'May . . . may I see the thunderbolt?'

Naso narrowed his eyes at Threptus, then shrugged and handed him the object in his hand.

'It's made of cloth!' said Threptus wonderingly. 'I thought it was metal! But it's gold cloth stuffed with something heavy and soft.'

'Couldn't make it real metal,' said Naso. 'Might kill someone if I missed. They use yellow cloth with a few gold threads in to make it shiny, then they stuff it with flour.'

'Why flour?' asked Threptus.

'To make the smoke. See here? This seam is loose. When the thunderbolt hits the stage it goes splat and the flour puffs up like smoke.'

'It goes splat and puff?'

'Yeah. Now get out of here before I make *you* go splat and puff.' He brought his spotty face close to Threptus and said, 'And I'm warning you, if any of my gang find out about this, I'll thump you.'

'I promise!' gasped Threptus. 'I won't tell!' He turned to open the door, but Naso gripped his arm. 'Not that way, blockhead! Go along the

83

back.' He pushed Threptus towards another door at the back of the room. Threptus found himself in a narrow high space full of ladders and scaffolding. He was behind the scaena! And there was Narcissus the famous pantomime dancer, binding his calf with a bandage. He looked up at Threptus. His eyes were rimmed with some kind of dark paint that made them startlingly blue.

'What do you want?' he said.

'Exit?' croaked Threptus.

Narcissus rolled his eyes and pointed. A few moments later, Threptus emerged at the extreme left of the stage into the vast bright cavea of the theatre. He scampered down the steps and started to make his way to the exit. He needed to go and see if Floridius was all right. Suddenly he saw a black-eyebrowed soldier up ahead. It was the same guard who had been with Bato and he was glaring at Threptus.

'Hey, you!' cried the guard. Threptus put up his hood, turned to go the other way, and bumped into the grey-haired lady in lavender!

'Oh!' she gasped. Then she caught his hand and called out to the guard, 'Don't worry; he's with me.'

Black Eyebrows scowled, but turned away.

'Stay close to me,' whispered the Lady in Lavender. 'I saw you yesterday in the forum and then again here at the pantomime. You love the theatre. Correct?'

Threptus nodded gratefully and let the Lady in Lavender guide him along the row past the knees of men in silk syntheses and women in fine woollen pallas. A fair-haired woman in an unbleached cloak smiled at him. There was a lavender cushion and a basket beside her.

'Squeeze in between me and my slave-girl Xenia,' said the Lady in Lavender, sitting on the cushion.

Xenia took the basket onto her lap so that Threptus could sit beside her.

'Today they are doing the story of Phaethon,' said the Lady in Lavender to Threptus. 'Do you know it?'

Threptus shook his head.

'Phaethon was the son of Helios, the sun

god. But he was a mortal, not a god. Despite this, he thought he could drive his father's chariot, the chariot of the sun. He was trying to be a god.'

'What happened?' asked Threptus.

'I won't spoil it for you,' said the Lady in Lavender with a smile. 'But the story shows the danger of playing god.' She turned to Xenia. 'What do we have for lunch?'

Xenia opened the basket. 'Slices of dry-cured beef, hard-boiled eggs and olives,' she replied.

The Lady in Lavender smiled at Threptus. 'There's far more here than the two of us can eat,' she said. 'Will you join us?'

Threptus's tummy growled and he nodded eagerly. He was ravenous, for he had only eaten an almond pastry shaped like a thunderbolt the day before.

For the next half hour they ate papyrus-thin slices of dry-cured beef, hard-boiled eggs dusted with cumin, and glossy purple olives from Greece. The food made Threptus thirsty, but Xenia had a wine skin of posca and the Lady in

Lavender did not seem to mind sharing it with him.

Then Bato made his announcement and the musicians began to play, and Narcissus leapt on stage to act out the story of Phaethon, son of Helios.

Threptus watched enthralled as Narcissus played the parts of Phaethon, Helios and even the two powerful horses hitched to the chariot of the sun. But Phaethon could not control the horses. They flew too high and plunged the lands below into snow and ice. They flew too low and scorched the earth. Finally Jupiter appeared on the dizzying heights of the backdrop and stopped Phaethon's disastrous ride with a thunderbolt.

Threptus swallowed hard. So that was what happened when you played god!

He looked at the Lady in Lavender. She was looking back at him, her chin down and her eyebrows raised.

'He killed him,' said Threptus. 'Jupiter killed Phaethon.'

The Lady in Lavender nodded sadly. 'Jupiter is never happy when mortals play god,' she said.

'But sometimes he will forgive you if you say you are sorry.'

At that moment Threptus had an idea of how he might make things right.

'MASTER!' WHISPERED THREPTUS AT the small slit of a window in a narrow alley between the Temple of Venus and the basilica. 'Master, are you there?'

'Threptus, me little friend! Is that you?'

'Yes, master. I brought you some food. Some slices of dry-cured beef and hard-boiled eggs and some purple olives.'

'I see the napkin! Push it through the slit. I can almost . . . Got it! Where did you get these things?'

'A nice lady at the theatre shared her seat and her lunch with me. I told her about you and she said I could take you their leftover food. She let me keep the napkin, too.'

'Praise the gods,' cried Floridius, 'for the kindness of strangers. How are things at home? Are me chickens still alive?'

'They're fine,' said Threptus. 'I've just been to see them. I cleaned their straw and topped up their water. They didn't eat anything but they walked around a little. Master, I have an idea of how to get you out, but it won't be until tomorrow. Will you be all right sleeping here tonight?'

'Yes, me little friend. Don't you worry. I have me woollen cloak. In fact, it's almost warmer down here than in our little shack, ha, ha! What's your plan?' he asked.

'I don't want to tell you in case it doesn't work, but will you pray to Jupiter?'

*

The third day of the Saturnalia, an hour before noon, Threptus stood outside the double doors of the house of the Pontifex Volcani and knocked. He wore his green paenula with the hood up and in his hand he carried a basket containing four figurines, three coloured chickens, his belled ankle-bangle and his panpipes.

As he waited for the door to open, he pulled the belled bangle over his foot and onto his ankle. It was probably a lady's bracelet but he had once seen his hero Lupus wearing something similar as an anklet. Later he'd found one in the necropolis rubbish dump and hoped it was the same one Lupus had worn. Just as he finished pulling it on, a big door-slave opened the door. He had not changed places with his master and he wore no Saturnalia cap. He glowered down at Threptus.

'Salve, O slave!' said Threptus politely. 'My name is Threptus and I am a soothsayer's apprentice. I know your master's daughter is ill and I think I know how to cure her.'

The big door slave turned his head. 'Master!' he shouted. 'There is a mini soothsayer at the door. He says he can cure Lucilia.'

Gamala appeared. 'Clamax! How many times have I told you? Don't bellow. Come to me with your message. Now what's this about mini soothsayers?' He glared down at Threptus.

Threptus took a deep breath. 'I think I can cure your daughter,' he said.

'What sort of cruel joke is this?' cried Gamala. 'My daughter is at the gates of Hades. I have tried every doctor in Ostia and none of them have been able to help. Go away!'

The double doors slammed shut and Threptus heard the bolt fall down.

Threptus closed his eyes. 'Please, Jupiter!' he prayed.

Then he took away the cloth covering the basket and let the three hens hop out. They were the three formerly white pullets, now pink, blue and green.

When he stamped his jangly ankle-bangle and blew his breathy panpipes, they began to strut in a circle around him.

'Bweerp, bweerp, bweerp!' they sang.

The brick walls of the narrow alley made the cheerful music sound loud and clear.

'Ecce, tata!' said a child's voice from above.

'Coloured chickens!' Threptus looked up at the apartment house balcony. A toddler in a little tunic and leggings was clapping his chubby hands in delight. Soon he was joined by his mother and older brother. From one of the other apartments emerged two girls about the same age as Threptus.

'Oh, they're so pretty!' cried one.

'They're dancing,' said the other.

Then Threptus saw a face appear in a small barred window of Gamala's house.

It was a pretty face: very pale and with a small mouth and big dark eyes swollen with weeping. Threptus was sure it was Lucilia. His plan was working!

'Thank you, Jupiter!' Threptus thought in his mind. But he played louder and stamped harder. He had learned one of the songs the pantomime players played. It was a happy, cheerful song.

By now a dozen people had crowded onto the apartment house balcony, more than half of them children. When he stopped playing they all applauded with cupped hands. They were giving him roof tiles!

Threptus felt his cheeks flush with pleasure.

It was time for the next step of his plan.

'Ladies and gentlemen, boys and girls . . . and Lucilia?' he looked up at the dark-haired girl.

She gave a tiny, frowning nod.

'I have come to tell you the Tale of the Soothsayer's Apprentice!' He tried to make his voice as loud as he could by shouting like Praeco the town crier. In the enclosed space of the alley it seemed to work.

From the basket he took out four figurines: a bronze Lar with a fluttery tunic, a chubby Bacchus made of wood and the two clay figurines of Jupiter and Juno.

'Once upon a time,' he began, 'there was a poor beggar boy named Threptus!' He made the bronze Lar walk across the muddy cobblestones. 'Threptus was often cold and damp, and always hungry!' The pink-dyed pullet wandered by and Threptus improvised, 'And sometimes he was chased by GIANT CHICKENS!' He made the Threptus figurine run away.

Up on the balcony, the children laughed.

'But one day,' continued Threptus, 'who should come to his rescue but a kind soothsayer named Floridius.'

Threptus made the Bacchus figurine come up to the Threptus figurine.

"'Do not fear, me little friend! I will take care of you. I will teach you how to read and write and look after some GIANT SACRED CHICKENS!'"

More laughter from the balcony.

'But one day,' proclaimed Threptus, 'a sad thing happened. The soothsayer and his apprentice did something bad. They played at being god. And Jupiter was angry!'

Here Threptus held up the little naked Jupiter.

"'Grrrr. I am angry! I am going to bring bad luck on the soothsayer and his apprentice and upon the GIANT SACRED CHICKENS! I am going to punish them for playing god! They tried to make the beautiful Lucilia marry the handsome Bato by stealing my thunder!'"

Threptus heard Lucilia gasp from the small window up above, but he hurried on.

"'No, dear husband,'" he made the Juno figurine say in a high-pitched lady's voice. "'Do not be too hard on the soothsayer and his apprentice. Do not throw them out of their humble shack abutting the Temple of Rome and Augustus. Do not take them away from their beloved GIANT CHICKENS. They only wanted to help the handsome Bato win the heart of the girl he loves. Show them mercy!"

"NO!" cried Jupiter. "No mercy! UNLESS the beautiful Lucilia will forgive them! Will you? Will you forgive the soothsayer and his apprentice?"' Threptus made the little clay Jupiter look up at the window.

But Lucilia had disappeared.

SCROLL XII

THREPTUS'S HEART SANK DOWN TO
his chilly toes. The children on the balcony
were applauding him, but Lucilia had stopped
watching from her window.

His plan had failed.

'Come on, Hera, Juno and Venus,' he said to
the pullets. 'Time to go.'

He packed the three pullets into the basket

along with the four figurines. He was turning to go when the chink of metal on cobbles brought him round. The people on the balcony were throwing coins!

He gathered up four little quadrans, an as and a dupondius. They did not even add up to one sestertius, but he knew it was a great deal of money for poor apartment dwellers.

Then he heard a girl's voice from behind Gamala's doors.

'Please, pater! Let me speak to him.'

Threptus quickly put the coins in his belt-pouch then turned to face the double doors as they swung open. There stood a slender girl in a pink woollen stola, holding a small dog. Her dark brown hair was loose around her shoulders. Her skin was pale and her big brown eyes were pink and swollen from crying.

Gamala and the big door slave stood behind her.

'Pater, I would like to speak to this boy in private.'

'But—'

'Please! It is my dying wish.'

Gamala sighed. 'Very well, Lucilia,' he said. 'How can I deny you a dying wish?'

Lucilia beckoned Threptus. Still clutching the basket of chickens, he went through the door and followed her upstairs. Her room was small but pretty, with scenes of Diana the huntress painted on the frescoed wall.

She pointed to a chair and when Threptus sat down she lay on the bed with her head on the pillow.

'I am dying,' she said, stroking her dog. 'So you must tell me the truth.'

Threptus put down the basket of chickens and nodded.

'Why did you make up that story about pretending to imitate thunder?'

'I didn't make it up,' said Threptus. 'That was fake thunder.'

'Impossible.' Lucilia put the back of her hand to her pale forehead. 'It was thunder from a clear sky,' she whispered. 'Three months ago it also thundered from a clear sky in Sabina. And the next day the emperor was dead. Now the same thing has happened to me. Jupiter is angry that I questioned his will.'

'I swear,' said Threptus, 'it wasn't Jupiter. It was me. I climbed up the vine outside your house and hung a big sheet of thin bronze called a thunder-sheet there, and when Floridius said the word I hit it with a wooden mallet. My master and I thought it would make you marry Bato, who loves you so much that just the thought of you makes him stutter. But then it fell down and made a big noise! The thunder-sheet was my idea, though, so you have to tell your father to let my master out of prison.' Threptus took a deep breath. 'You can put me in prison instead of him.'

Lucilia closed her eyes and shook her head. 'You're just saying that to cheer me up. I can tell the difference between thunder and a rattling sheet of bronze.'

'Come with me to the theatre,' said Threptus. 'I'll prove it to you.'

Lucilia opened her eyes. 'Pater does not permit me to go to the theatre or anywhere else,' she said. 'He says it is not dignified for the Chief Priest's daughter.'

'You've never been to the theatre?' said Threptus. 'Or seen a farce in the forum?'

'No,' she said. 'I only go to the Baths of Artemis once a week with my aunt and my slave-girl.'

'Then you must come to the theatre.'

Lucilia turned her head and regarded him with her big brown eyes. 'But I'm dying! I can feel my strength fading.'

'Then we have to hurry!'

Lucilia hugged her little dog. 'But if one of pater's clients were to see me at the theatre, it would be a terrible disgrace for him.'

'Wear a disguise!' cried Threptus.

'What do you mean?'

Threptus thought hard.

When I go downstairs,' he said. 'I'll tell your father that you are sleeping and want to be left alone. Then I'll let the chickens loose in the courtyard and pretend they escaped. When everyone comes to help me catch them, you slip outside and wait round the corner. Then we'll trade clothes!'

Lucilia sat up. 'Isn't that nefas?'

Threptus shook his head. 'It's not forbidden. It's the Saturnalia, when everything is allowed!'

'Oh!' she whispered. 'My heart is beating fast at the thought!'

'Are you afraid?'

'Yes.'

'Are you more afraid of going to the theatre than of dying?'

She looked at him for a moment, her dark eyes huge. He noticed her pale cheeks were pink.

Finally she nodded. 'All right,' she whispered. 'I'll do it!'

W HILE THE HIGH PRIEST AND HIS
slave Clamax were searching the
bushes for the three colourful pullets, Threptus
ran to the double doors and let himself
out. Lucilia was waiting round the corner,
wrapped in her fringed pink palla.

Threptus smiled at her. 'Take my
green woollen paenula,' he said, pulling it

off and handing it to her. 'And I'll wear your palla.'

She gasped. 'But then you'll look like a little girl, and I'll look like a boy!'

'I told you,' said Threptus, 'it's the Saturnalia. Everything is upside-down and topsy-turvy. Yesterday I saw a lady and her slave-girl trade places.'

Reluctantly, Lucilia gave Threptus her palla and took his cloak. She did up the boar's-tooth toggle and pulled the hood up over her loose dark hair.

'Take off your earrings,' he said. 'Good. And just hike up your stola so your legs show.'

'My legs?' she squeaked. 'But that's scandalous! I've never even shown my legs to pater.'

'Here!' Threptus reached inside the cloak and tugged up her stola above the belt, making it blouse out and raising the hem to just below her knees. There was only a hand span of it showing beneath the paenula.

'Oh,' gasped Lucilia. 'My legs feel so cold and strange.'

'They look wrong, too,' murmured Threptus. 'They're too white and smooth. Wait . . .'

He bent down and rubbed his hand in some mud between the paving stones. He used this to streak her calves.

'Oh!' cried Lucilia. 'It tickles!

'That's better,' said Threptus, standing up and brushing his hands together. 'Now, try walking like this.' He stomped forwards on flat feet. 'And I'll walk like this.' He pulled her pink palla over his head and sashayed along, swaying his hips.

Lucilia giggled.

'See,' he said. 'That's what the Saturnalia is all about. Fun and laughter. Slaves dressed as masters. Girls dressed as boys. Now come on, or we'll never get a good seat for the pantomime!'

As they passed through the crowded forum, Lucilia whispered, 'I feel invisible! Usually people stare at me when I go to the baths. I can never look at them because they're looking at me. Oh!' she cried. 'Was that thunder?'

'No,' grinned Threptus. 'That was a comic actor called Crepitus. He makes that noise with his bottom.'

Lucilia looked at him wide-eyed. Then she covered her mouth to stifle another giggle.

They made their way up the crowded Decumanus Maximus. Threptus had to keep tugging Lucilia's hand. She wanted to stop and watch some dancing girls and buy a spiced sausage from Brutus's stall and listen to a poet on a corner. He was reciting a funny poem about a priest of Jupiter who offended the Thunderer by breaking wind during a sacrfice:

A priest stood on the Capitoline Hill.
He bowed and scraped with all his will.
He prayed to Jupiter with all his heart
Suddenly his bottom made a great big—

'Come on!' cried Threptus. 'Or we won't get a good seat!'

As they joined the stream of people filing through the vaulted entrance of the theatre, Lucilia kept making the sign against evil. 'Pater always told me wicked things happen at shows,' she whispered to Threptus. 'He said if I ever went to the theatre or the arena I must stop up my ears and close my —Oh!'

They had just emerged into the theatre.

'Look at it!' breathed Lucilia. 'And look at all the people! Where will we sit?'

Threptus felt like an expert. 'Up there,' he said. He intended to go right up to the top, but then he saw two empty places seven rows up. Boldly he took Lucilia's hand and led her along the row. They sat down between a fat man and the priest of Hercules.

'Oh!' cried Lucilia. 'Someone bumped my back with their knees!' Then she giggled.

'Don't giggle,' hissed Threptus. 'You're supposed to be a boy!'

In front of him the Lady in Lavender turned her head and he saw the curve of her eye for just a moment. He lowered his head and pulled his palla around his face. Luckily he was disguised as a little girl in pink.

The Lady in Lavender turned back as Marcus Artorius Bato stepped out onto the stage.

Before the young magistrate could open his mouth, everyone cheered.

'Is that Bato?' Lucilia whispered in Threptus's ear.

Threptus nodded. 'He's the sponsor.'

'Everyone's cheering him!'

'He's very popular,' said Threptus.

When Bato had finished introducing the pantomime, which was to be the story of Aeneas and Lavinia, Lucilia bent her head again. 'He doesn't stammer when he's speaking to lots of people,' she said.

'Until the day before yesterday,' said Threptus, 'I'd never heard Bato stammer.'

'He stammers all the time when he's with me!'

Threptus said, 'That's because he loves you.'

'He doesn't love me,' Lucilia tossed her head and had to straighten the hood. 'He's only marrying me because pater told him to.'

'No!' Threptus had to shout to make himself heard, for the crowds were still cheering Bato. 'I overheard him once. Bato really loves you.'

The last words sounded too loud, for the crowd had grown instantly silent as the musicians started to play.

Everyone in the rows nearby turned to stare at Threptus.

He gave them a sheepish grin and shrugged. The Lady in Lavender stared at him the longest. Then she twisted to look at Lucilia, then looked back at Threptus in his pink palla. Suddenly her eyes grew wide. She had recognised him! But when she tapped the side of her nose and gave him a smiling wink, he knew she would keep his secret. He smiled back and gave her a relieved thumbs-up.

Another roar of applause filled the marble shell of the theatre as Narcissus somersaulted out onto the stage. For the next two hours Threptus forgot everything apart from the story.

It was the best story yet: the story of the ageing warrior Aeneas, and Lavinia, the beautiful sixteen-year-old princess who finally won his heart. They would become the great, great grandparents of the Romans.

Narcissus danced the story wearing a double-sided mask, playing both parts in turn.

Near the end, a rumble of thunder followed

by a crash made everyone gasp and Lucilia jumped.

'Don't you worry, son,' said the man sitting next to Lucilia. 'It's not real thunder. See the musician down there in front of the stage? He made that noise by rubbing that sheet of bronze with a mallet and then hitting it.'

Lucilia nodded silently, but Threptus saw that her face was white.

The fake thunder came again in a great resounding crash. This time Lucilia gasped, and smiled.

'Is that really how you made the thunder yesterday?' she said in Threptus's ear.

He nodded.

'So Jupiter wasn't angry with me for turning down Bato?'

Threptus shook his head. 'Jupiter wasn't angry. It was a fake thunder omen.'

Hanno banged the bronze thunder-sheet a third time.

Lucilia laughed and applauded with everyone else, then pointed up. 'Oh, look!' Up on the balcony stood a turquoise-robed figure with slim hips, a large bust and a woman's mask. It was Venus, mother of Aeneas and of the Roman race, and goddess of love.

Or was it?

'It's Naso!' whispered Threptus to himself. 'He's wearing fake bosom padding! And then out loud, 'Eureka! I solved the mystery!'

'What mystery?'

'The mystery of why somebody told me and my friends never to come to the theatre. He dresses up as goddesses!'

'Who cares?' said Lucilia gaily. 'It's the Saturnalia when anything is allowed and I'm not going to die!'

They both clapped enthusiastic roof tiles as Narcissus and his troupe took a bow.

'Oh, Threptus!' exclaimed Lucilia as the crowd rose to go. 'That was the most wonderful thing I've ever seen. I can't believe I'm sixteen and have never seen a pantomime. Are there other sorts of stories?'

'Yes,' said Threptus, standing up with the others. 'Lots of other stories. Plus there are farces, comedies and tragedies. But the best are pantomimes. Bato is sponsoring one every day of this holiday.'

'Eheu!' said Lucilia as they started to file along the seats towards the aisle. 'Oh, no!'

'What's wrong?' asked Threptus.

'Those soldiers are looking right at me. Pater must have discovered my absence.'

Threptus turned to see a pair of soldiers standing by the right hand exit of the theatre. Bato was talking to one of them. The other was looking in their direction.

'See?' said Lucilia. 'That one with the big, black eyebrows is looking right at me!'

'No he's not,' said Threptus. 'He's looking right at me!' He grabbed Lucilia's hand.

'Keep your head down and follow me!' he hissed over his shoulder. He followed the stream of people as they shuffled along the row. When the people in this front section reached an aisle, they all turned to go down shallow steps towards the orchestra. But Threptus pulled Lucilia up the stairs against the flow of the crowd towards the upper tier. People jostled and pushed them. Some glared, others muttered curses.

Threptus kept repeating, 'Excuse us, excuse us!'

Finally they reached the middle section of the cavea. The audience in this section was funnelled up towards arched doorways with stairs leading back down to the shops on the Decumanus Maximus. Already this section of the theatre was nearly empty.

'Quickly!' cried Threptus over his shoulder. 'Make for the vomitorium!'

'The what?'

Threptus grinned. 'It's just a fancy word for "entrance" or "exit". My mentor taught me that!'

'Ugh!' she said. 'It sounds like a room where people go to vomit.'

But as they reached the vomitorium, Threptus saw a pair of soldiers coming up the stairs, pushing through the last of the people going out.

'Change of plan!' gasped Threptus. 'Back the way we came!'

As they hurried back down the awkward half-steps, Threptus almost tripped on the fringe of his long pink palla. When they reached the orchestra he grabbed Lucilia's hand and pulled her towards the arch of the central exit. But he skidded to a halt when he saw two guards silhouetted against the bright main street at the far end.

There were guards in both the side exits, too.

Then he remembered there were ways out on either side of the stage.

'Run!' he whispered over his shoulder. 'Up on stage! Once we're out of here we can take off our disguises. That will fool them!'

Behind him, Lucilia was making a strange sobbing noise.

He glanced back, expecting to see her eyes swollen and red with fresh tears. He was astonished to discover that she was laughing.

'What are you laughing about?' he gasped.

'I've never run before!'

'You've never run?'

'Not since I was about six. It's fun isn't it?'

'Yes!' laughed Threptus. 'It's fun!'

They scrambled up the steps to the stage.

'That way!' cried Threptus, pointing stage left. 'We can get out that way.'

They started running to the left-hand side of the stage when suddenly a figure appeared, blocking their escape. The soldier's big, black eyebrows were scrunched down in a fierce glare.

'I'll teach you kids,' he growled.

SCROLL XIV

S PLAT! A GOLDEN OBJECT FELL FROM above, striking the soldier squarely on the helmet. It was Jupiter's thunderbolt! The flour puffed out in a big cloud and hid him from view for a moment.

Threptus and Lucilia looked up to see a masked figure on the dizzying heights of the backdrop. Big-breasted Venus gave them a thumbs-up and Threptus heard a voice say, 'You owe me a favour, me old son.'

Threptus could not believe it. The bully Naso had come to his rescue!

The Saturnalia really was a topsy-turvy time of year.

'This way!' cried Lucilia, grasping his hand. 'Out the other vomitorium!' She turned and ran back across the stage.

Straight into the arms of Ostia's duumvir.

Lucilia squealed as her hood fell back and her hair tumbled down. She tried to pull away but the magistrate had her firmly in his grip.

'Bato!' exclaimed Threptus.

'Bato!' boomed Venus from up above.

'Bato!' squealed Lucilia.

'Lucilia!' Bato's pale brown eyes opened in astonishment. 'Is that you?'

She nodded.

He let her go and she took a step back.

He looked her up and down. 'What are you doing here dressed like that?'

She gave him a radiant smile. 'I came to see the pantomime. Dressing like a boy was the only way I could get out of the house.'

She tugged off Threptus's green paenula and handed it to him, then accepted her own pink palla and pulled it around her shoulders. 'Exchanging clothes was Threptus's idea.'

'You are friends with the soothsayer's apprentice?'

She nodded. 'He convinced me to come to the pantomime. It was my first time and I loved it.'

'You did?' Bato's voice was husky.

'Oh, Marcus,' she breathed. 'I loved it! I could watch a pantomime every single day of my life.'

Bato swallowed hard. 'Really?'

She nodded. 'And you! You spoke so well, even though everyone was looking at you. Why didn't you stutter?' She tipped her head to one side. 'You stuttered when you met me last week.'

Bato's ears were pink. 'That's be-be-be—'

'Because he was nervous,' said a woman's voice. 'Marcus only stutters when he's nervous, don't you, darling?'

They all three turned to see the grey-haired Lady in Lavender coming up the steps. Her slave-girl hurried behind.

'Mater!' cried Bato. 'You're supposed to be looking after our villa in Comum. What are you doing here in Ostia?'

'Celebrating the Saturnalia, of course,' she said. 'Plus a little bird told me you were thinking of getting engaged. Is this the lucky girl?'

'No,' said Bato, staring at the ground. 'She—'

'Shhh!' said Lucilia, pressing her finger to his lips. 'Don't say anything yet.'

The tips of Bato's ears grew pink again. 'You mean I st-st-still have a chance?'

'You're Bato's mother?' asked Threptus, his eyes wide.

Lady Lavender inclined her head. 'Marcia Artoria,' she said. 'How do you do?'

Threptus nodded, too.

Lucilia stepped forward with a radiant smile. 'I am Lucilia Gamala,' she said. 'Daughter of the Pontifex Volcani. Your son and I are betrothed. If,' she added, 'he promises to let me see a pantomime every day.'

Threptus tugged her palla and when she bent down he whispered in her ear.

'And if,' Lucilia added, 'he releases Floridius

the Soothsayer from prison and gives him one hundred sesterces!'

*

Threptus in the port of Ostia to Lupus in the port of Ephesus:

Greetings, friend! This week was the Saturnalia. My master and I tried to do good by helping arrange a betrothal between a magistrate named Bato and a beautiful girl named Lucilia. But when we made a fake thunder omen it all went wrong. Jupiter punished us for playing god. But I said sorry to Jupiter and confessed everthing to Lucilia and now she and Bato are engaged. Yesterday my master and I went to their betrothal feast at the house of Publius Lucilius Gamala. Floridius let Lucilia keep three dancing pullets as a present. (She has promised never to eat them.) Just as the ceremony was finishing there was a big clap of thunder! Lucilia screamed because she doesn't like thunder, but Floridius came to the rescue. He said he had been reading his Etruscan Almanac and thunder on that day meant there would be 'a disease for men, but a harmless one'. Bato had his arms around Lucilia and he said that Floridius's book must be right because he had a disease harmless to men and that it was called 'LOVE'. Then Lucilia laughed and kissed Bato IN FRONT OF EVERYONE! After that I played my panpipes and the coloured pullets did their chicken dance.

P.S. We have a new roof and a GLASS SKYLIGHT and everything is warm and cosy. Yo, Saturnalia!

THE ROMAN MYSTERY SCROLLS

Find out how the adventures began in . . .

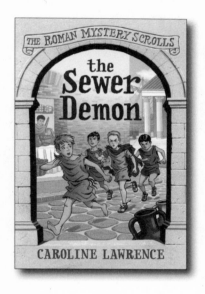

Threptus, once a beggar boy in the
Ancient Roman port of Ostia, has joined
forces with Floridius – freelance soothsayer,
and dealer in sacred chickens. Now he finds
himself struggling to outwit the law, solve
mysteries and even fight 'demons'!

The adventure continues in . . .

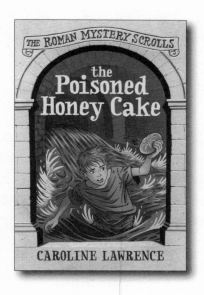

Floridius, freelance soothsayer,
is afraid that he has lost his talent for
seeing the future. Threptus wants to
find some titbits of information that his
mentor can use to convince people he still
has the gift, but will a poisoned honey
cake lead to disaster along the way?

the
orion star

Sign up for **the orion star**
newsletter to get inside information
about your favourite children's authors
as well as exclusive competitions and
early reading copy giveaways.

www.orionbooks.co.uk/newsletters

Orion
Children's Books